For Lucy

First edition for the United States, Canada, and the Philippines
published 1988 by Barron's Educational Series

Text © copyright 1988 by John Greaves
Illustrations © copyright 1988 by Edward McLachlan

First published in Great Britain in 1988 by Methuen Children's Books Ltd.
London, England

All inquiries should be addressed to:
Barron's Educational Series, Inc.
250 Wireless Boulevard
Hauppauge, New York 11788

Library of Congress Catalog Card No. 87-19580
International Standard Book No. 0-8120-6090-3

Library of Congress Cataloging-in-Publication Data

Greaves, John.
  Henrietta the clumsy hippo.

  Summary: Henrietta the clumsy Hippo wreaks
havoc with her careless dancing, until one of
the other animals makes a wise suggestion.
  [1. Hippopotamus – Fiction.   2. Animals –
Fiction.   3. Dancing – Fiction.   4. Clumsiness –
Fiction.]   I. McLachlan, Edward.   II. Title.
PZ7.G79994He 1988 [E]   87-19580
ISBN 0-8120-6090-3

Printed in Italy

890   987654321

HENRIETTA
The Clumsy Hippo

John Greaves and Edward McLachlan

BARRON'S
New York · Toronto

More than anything
Henrietta wanted to dance,

but being a hippo she was a little on the
large side and rather inclined to be clumsy.

Every morning Henrietta would put on her ballet shoes
and leap away into the forest, knocking over trees,
treading on folks' tails, and causing havoc around the
water hole where she lived.

One day all the other animals decided they had had
enough of being trodden on, and they gathered for a
meeting in a clearing in the forest.

There was a crocodile nursing a bandaged tail, an
ostrich, a pair of monkeys holding each other up and
lots of other animals, all with a complaint to make
about Henrietta Hippo.

The committee chairman, a stern-looking vulture, was making a speech about respecting other people's property when Henrietta spun into the clearing.

All the animals leaped for cover, but the crocodile was too slow. Henrietta did a grand leap and landed on the poor croc's tail.

"The committee has decided
it will have to stop,"
said the vulture.

"What will?" asked
Henrietta, stooping to tighten
the bows of her shoe.

"This reckless disregard
for other people's property,
not to mention their tails,"
replied the vulture sternly.

"We are going to confiscate your ballet shoes, Henrietta."

"But I won't be able to dance anymore," said Henrietta sadly.

"That's the idea," hissed the crocodile.

Henrietta wandered through the forest. She did not notice the sun go down or the moon come up.

She was so miserable she did not even notice the old
tree until . . . bang – she walked straight into it!

"Hey, watch where you're going," said a voice, and a fruit bat climbed out of the hole that Henrietta had knocked him into. "You really ought to watch where you are going."

"I am sorry," said Henrietta sadly, "but I have always been a rather clumsy Hippo." And she told the bat all about her dancing and the committee's decision.

The bat thought very hard.

"Henrietta," he said after a while, "I think I may have a solution for you. Without wishing to be rude you *are* a little heavy to go leaping around the jungle, but if you were to dance underwater you would appear much lighter. You could dance all day and not worry anyone."

Henrietta was thrilled.
She leaped up and gave the
bat a big kiss, knocking
him back into his hole.
Then she ran as fast as
her fat little legs would
carry her until she
reached the water hole.

As soon as it was light out, Henrietta stood by the edge, took a deep breath and did a spectacular leap into the water.

She stood on the bottom of the water hole, bent her knees and launched herself into one of her grand leaps

Gracefully she floated through the water and landed
about twenty feet away.

"My goodness," thought Henrietta. "That was rather
good, and not a damaged tail in sight."

All afternoon Henrietta danced,
completely unaware that a large
crowd was gathering.
When she eventually stopped
the crowd went mad. There were
cries of "Marvelous", "Such
grace", and "More, More".

The news that
a very graceful Hippo
had been seen
dancing underwater
spread quickly.
Animals flocked from
far and wide
to see her perform.

Henrietta visited water holes all over the jungle to make guest appearances, but she always returned to her own little water hole where she was now known as Henrietta the Dancing Hippo.